Francis Sharp in the Grip of the Uncanny!

Chapter 1

LOCKH
McFRY'S STRANGE FICTION MONTHLY, JUNE 1933
THE OCCULTIST IN "THE ADIRONDACKS MAN-APE"
IN THE DEEP WOODS OF NEW YORK STATE,
FRESHWATER MERMAIDS OF M
VLVAN
EVIL
RAIL OF
ALACHIA
IAL
SITING
LANCA
GNOME CITY
AL
PHILADE
MOTH WOMAN OF WEST VIRGINIA
UNDERGROUND GNOME CITY!!
OCCULTIST FIGHTS GNOME KING.
PINE B
THE OCCULTIS
THE JERSEY
DELEWARE DEMON HOUNDS
MORE
NTAIN
OLLS

NEW YORK
OF SECRET CULT
Witch Woods OF JERSEY
WEST MILFORD
NEW YORK city
Occultist Finds THE GEM OF the ORIENT
WESTFIELD
CAMP
DOVER
JERSEY CITY
NEW YORK CITY
EDISON
TRENTON
N
W
E
S
NEW JERSEY
VINELAND
ATLANTIC CITY

Francis Sharp in the Grip of the Uncanny!

Chapter 1

DRAWN BY BRITTNEY SABO AND CO-AUTHORED BY ANNA BRATTON

SPECIAL THANKS TO THE XERIC FOUNDATION FOR PROVIDING THE FUNDS TO PRINT THIS BOOK.

PRINTED BY MCNAUGHTON & GUNN
SALINE, MICHIGAN

FIRST EDITION, OCTOBER 2010

WWW.BSABO.COM

ISBN: 978-0-9776616-8-8

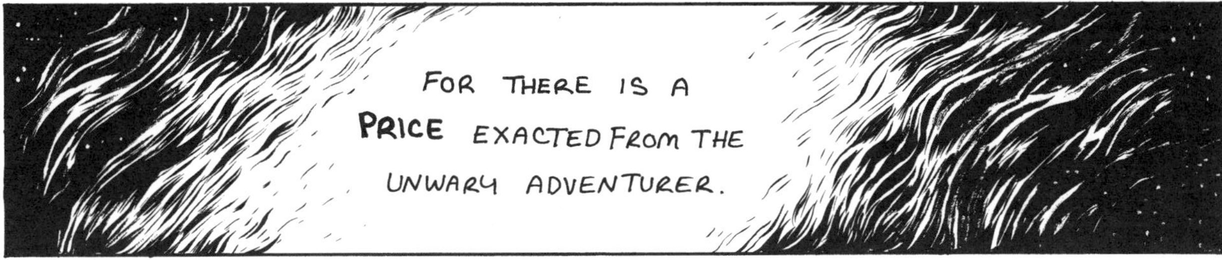

THE UNKNOWN IS NOT FORGIVING TO THOSE WHO TRESPASS IN THE HOLY PLACES OF MYSTERY -

JOIN US, THEN—
AS WE EXPLORE THE WASTES OF THE ENIGMATIC—

AS WE TRAVEL TO THE FURTHEST STARS—
FRANCIS?

FRANCIS!
AS WE DUEL WITH DEMONS AND SUP WITH GHOSTS—

I SAID I'LL DO IT!
YOU SAID THAT HALF AN HOUR AGO.
BUT MY SHOWS ARE ON!
CLICK!
TELL THAT TO THE COWS! GO, FRANCIS.
AS WE HAGGLE WITH...

BUT I WANTED TO HEAR THAT!
IT'S ENOUGH THAT THOSE SERIALS MAKE YOU EXCITABLE AND YOU'LL BE UP WITH NIGHTMARES.

HORRIBLE STORIES.
I AIN'T SCARED.

NICE YOUNG MEN SHOULDN'T HAVE ANYTHING TO DO WITH THAT GARBAGE.
BUT-
FRANCIS, MIND YOUR MOTHER.

NOW, I NEED YOU TO TAKE THE COWS OUT TO THE PASTURE FOR A WHILE.
A CHUNK OF THE FENCE STILL NEEDS MENDING, SO-

SO? THE COWS WON'T GO ANYWHERE.
THEY'LL HEAD TO THE NEIGHBORS, FIRST CHANCE.
LOOK, JUST KEEP AN EYE ON THEM UNTIL I CAN GET UP THERE, ALL RIGHT?

STUPID COWS.

WHAT WAS THAT?

NOTHING...

YAWN...

Hmmm...

THE UNKNOWN IS NOT FORGIVING TO THOSE WHO TRESPASS IN THE HOLY PLACES OF MYSTERY-

COME WITH US THEN-

INTO THE WORLD OF-

BUM-
BUM-
BUMMM
!!!

THE OCCULTIST!

AHA! MY VILE NEM-NEME- . . .
HISSSSS!
AHA! MY VILE ENEMY, THE REVENANT!

HISSSSSSS
I SHALL DEFEAT YOU OCCULTIST!!

FIEND! YOU'LL NOT SUCCEED IN THIS WORLD OR THE NEXT!
PUT UP YER DUKES!

I AM THE WORLD'S FIRST AND BEST DEFENSE AGAINST THE FORCES OF EVIL, REVENANT!

TO FIGHT ME IS TO GRAPPLE WITH GENIUS!
MUNCH
MUNCH
MUNCH

I'LL GET YOU FOR THIS, OCCULTIST!
MACPHEARSON
BEST
BLUEBERRIES & PRODUCE

I'LL TAN YOUR BACKSIDE, BOY!
DIDN'T I **TELL** YOU TO MIND THOSE COWS?!

I WAS!
THEY JUST... GOT AWAY! THERE'S A BUNCHA' THEM, JUST ONE OF ME, AND THEY HEARD THIS NOISE-

YOU WEREN'T **WATCHING.**
I WAS.

NOW JUST **CALM** DOWN, THOMAS.
MR. MACPHEARSON SAID THEY DIDN'T RUIN **TOO** MUCH, BUT HE'S THINKING OF PRESSING CHARGES IF WE CAN'T PAY HIM BACK-

DAMNATION!
WATCH YOUR LANGUAGE!

THEY DIDN'T EVEN EAT THAT MUCH!
WHY'S THIS MY FAULT?
HE WAS COUNTING ON THAT CROP, FRANCIS.

IT'S BEEN A LEAN YEAR FOR FARMERS–

AND NOW IT'S GOTTEN LEANER.
I'D SEND YOU OVER THERE TO WORK OFF THE DEBT–
'CEPT YOU'D LIKELY RACK UP A WHOLE NEW SET OF CHARGES...
ISN'T MY BUSINESS TO RUN THIS FARM...

FRANCIS MARTIN SHARP, GO TO YOUR ROOM, THIS INSTANT!
I'M EATIN'!
FRANCIS!!

...A HUNDRED DOLLARS, MOSTLY JUST WANTS THE FENCE FIXED...
...I'M STILL GETTING THE WEST FENCE UP. TAKIN' FOREVER...
OCCULTIST

ONE BY THE OF NEXT WEEK-
COULDN'T AFFORD 'EM.
I WISH WE COULD'VE KEPT THE FARMHANDS-
BUT FRANCIS JUST WON'T HELP OUT-

THINKS HE'S TOO CLEVER BY HALF.
AND HIS **LAZINESS** AND HIS **LYING**-
THAT BOY NEEDS TO CHANGE, AND THAT'S GONNA HAPPEN, ONE WAY OR THE OTHER.

THE BANK'S COMING FOR US AS IS, THOMAS.
WE'RE NOT LICKED YET. WHEN WE GO INTO TOWN TOMORROW, WE'LL SELL SOME THINGS-
THE OLD STOVE-
THE PAINTED SCREEN, THE SILVER-

SIGH
MY PA'S WATCH...
!!!

- AN UNENDING VISTA OF RUIN AND DESPAIR FOR THESE AND OTHER FARM FAMILIES, WITH NO SIMPLE SOLUTION, IF ANY.-
WELL, IT'S COMING UP TO 7:45 AM AND IT'LL BE WHATLEY COFFEE THEATRE HOUR NEXT -
ARGH! HURRY UP!

SWEETIE? ARE YOU UP?
YEAH, MA!
ARE YOU LISTENING TO THAT RADIO?
NO, MA!

ARE YOU EATING IN THE SITTING ROOM? I DON'T WANT YOU EATING IN-
NO, MA!
SCOOT

- BY THE MINDS BEHIND THE BEST WEIRD FICTION BEING WRITTEN TODAY, AND YOU'RE IN FOR A TREAT, FOLKS.
ALRIGHT!
EQUAL PARTS MYSTERY AND HORROR-

- WITH A TOUCH OF PULSE-POUNDING ROMANCE -
EW.

AND OF COURSE, MURDER AND MAYHEM-
NOW WE'RE TALKING!

ADAPTED FOR RADIO, IT'S A FULL CAST PRODUCTION OF "THOSE DISTANT CLOCKWORK SHOR-
HEY!

IT'S GOING ON THE TRUCK, FRANCIS.
WHAT?!

WE GOT DEBTS TO PAY.
AND YOUR FOOLISHNESS YESTERDAY DIDN'T HELP US NONE.
BUT-

BUT YOU CAN'T! WHAT'LL WE LISTEN TO? WHAT ABOUT THE NEWS?
WE STILL GET THE PAPER.

BUT MY PROGRAMS -
- HAVE CAUSED YOU **ENOUGH** TROUBLE. TIME YOU PAID ATTENTION TO LEARNING HOW A FARM'S RUN.

NOT GONNA BE A FARMER-

ANYWAY, SCHOOL STARTS IN TWO WEEKS
THANK GOD.
DEAR!
?

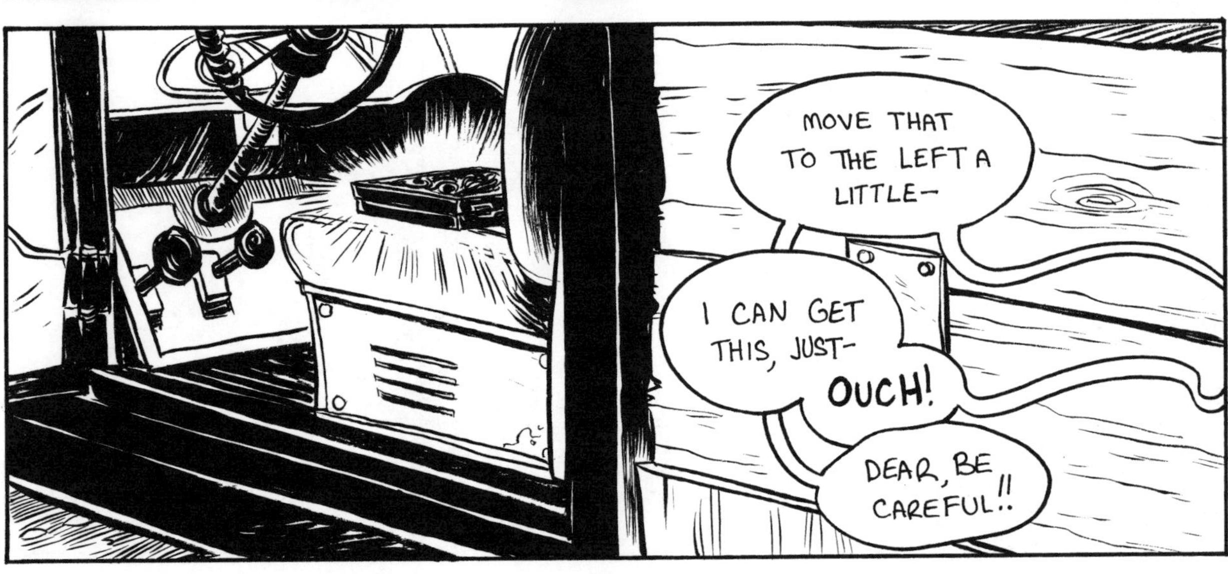
MOVE THAT TO THE LEFT A LITTLE-
I CAN GET THIS, JUST-
OUCH!
DEAR, BE CAREFUL!!

NO, TURN IT SIDEWAYS-

I CAN MOVE THE SILVERWARE TO THE FRONT-

FRANCIS!

Y-YESSIR?

FRONT AND CENTER. WE'RE GOIN' INTO TOWN-
HOT DOG!
NOT YOU. YOUR MA AND ME.

AWWWW!
YOU STILL HAVE CHORES, FRANCIS.
COWS ARE MILKED, BUT THE GARDEN STILL NEEDS WEEDING.

BUT I'LL MIND, HONEST!
YOU ALWAYS SAY THAT.
NOW HERE'S A CHANCE TO PROVE IT BY LOOKING AFTER THINGS.

JUST SIT TIGHT 'TIL WE'RE BACK FROM WESTFIELD.

SUPPER'S IN THE ICE BOX. WE'LL BE BACK LATE.
COULD YOU AT LEAST BRING ME BACK SOME PENNY CANDY?
SON, YOU JUST COUNT YOURSELF LUCKY IF YOU EVEN GET NEW SHOES THIS YEAR.

BEDTIME IS 7:30!
DON'T FORGET TO BRUSH YOUR TEETH-

The Occultist in The Mask of Eternity
The Occultist in The Sands of Time

HELLOOO?
ANYBODY HOME?

HEY, HARRY.

HI, FRANCIS!
IS IT STARTED YET?
UHH...

THEY GOT RID OF YOUR RADIO?!
AW, FRANCIS! I WALKED FOUR MILES FOR THIS!
YOU LIVE TWO MILES AWAY.
WORKS OUT TO FOUR, THERE AND BACK.

NOW WE'LL NEVER KNOW HOW THE CURSE OF KING SEMERKHET WAS LIFTED...
...HAVE TO ASK THAT RAT FINK JIM O'LEARY HOW IT ENDS.
STUPID TOWNIE.
AT LEAST IT WASN'T ONE OF THE BETTER STORIES-

WHAT?! IT WAS GREAT!
I COULDN'T FIGURE OUT WHAT WAS GOING ON-

YOU KNOW, PARALLEL DIMENSIONS!
"CRACKS IN THE PLASTER OF REALITY"-
YEAH, BUT WHAT DOES THAT EVEN MEAN?

WH- IT MEANS THINGS LIKE BIGFOOT AND THE JERSEY DEVIL MAKE SENSE!!
NO SUCH THINGS.
YEAH, BUT IF THERE WAS-
THERE ISN'T!
OKAY, BUT IF THERE-

ANYWAY, THE GHOST STORIES WERE BETTER.
GUESS WE WON'T HEAR THOSE NOW, EITHER.
SO NOW WHAT DO WE DO?
WELL...

WE MEET AGAIN, REVENANT!

OCCULTIST! HOW DARE YOU-
SAY "THE OCCULTIST"
I DID!

NO, YOU SAID "OCCULTIST."
SAME THING. ANYWAY, YOU DIDN'T SAY "THE REVENANT."

THE EYE OF MITHRIDATES WILL HOLD YOU TO THE TRUTH!
HEY! THAT'S YOUR PA'S WATCH!
YEAH, SORTA. ANYWAY-

HOW COME YOU'VE GOT IT?
JUST DO.
BESIDES, GRANDPA PROMISED IT TO ME.
WHERE'S YOUR OLD TALISMAN?
MA TOOK IT AWAY AFTER I BROKE THAT MIRROR...

ANYWAY.
I'VE STUMBLED ONTO YOUR DIABOLICAL PLAN-
POW! TAKE THAT!

NO, YOU HAVE TO EXPLAIN YOUR PLAN FIRST.
WHY? NOBODY DOES THAT.
THE REVENANT DOES!

REAL BAD GUYS DON'T DO THAT.
I BET AT LEAST SOME DO.

WHY DO WE ALWAYS PLAY OCCULTIST? IT'S BORING!
IT'S NOT!
ANYWAY, YOU KEEP COMING OVER!
LET'S PLAY COWBOYS AND INJUNS.
AT LEAST THEY'RE REAL.

COWBOYS DON'T SAVE THE WORLD.
AND THEY DON'T SAVE PEOPLE, OR FIGHT EVIL-
OR BATTLE NECROMANTIC HARPY-WOMEN!

ALL THE OCCULTIST IS ABOUT IS ONE DEAD GUY FIGHTING OTHER DEAD GUYS!!
YEAH, 'COS HE DOESN'T KILL THE LIVING!
"I ONLY KILL PEOPLE-
-WHO ARE ALREADY DEAD."
THAT DOESN'T EVEN MAKE SENSE.

HE DOES THAT BECAUSE HE HAS TO PROTECT HUMANITY-

- FROM ELDRITCH HORROR FROM BEYOND!!
ZZZZZTT

ANYWAY, COWBOYS ARE KID STUFF.
I'M GOIN' HOME.

C'MON!
WE ALWAYS PLAY THE OCCULTIST!
YEAH, AFTER WE LISTEN TO IT.
AND IT'S NOT LIKE WE'RE GONNA DO THAT ANYMORE.

WELL, WE CAN DO SOMETHING ELSE-
LIKE WHAT?
AND DON'T SAY "PLAY THE SHAD- "

WAIT!

LOOK... OVER THERE...

SOMETHING'S THERE NEXT TO THAT TREE. SEE IT?
PROBABLY A RACCOON OR THE-
MROW

-CAT.
MROW

MROW

MROW
!!!
TIME TO INVESTIGATE!

FRANCIS!

FRANCIS! WAIT UP!
IT'S GETTING AWAY!

FRANCIS!

FRANCIS!

WE SHOULDN'T GO ANY FURTHER. C'MON...
WHAT? ARE YOU SCARED?

WHAT IF THERE ARE **HOBOS** OR **ROBBERS** CAMPING OUT HERE?!
ROBBERS?
YOU **ARE** SCARED.

NO...
BUT IT GETS CREEPY DEEP IN-

WHAT?
WAIT UP!

WE'RE LOSING IT!!

FRANCIS!
FRANCIS! HELP!

WHAT IS IT?!
I CAN'T- I CAN'T-
I'M STUCK!

I CAN'T GET LOOSE! HELP!
...

DON'T LEAVE ME ALONE WITH THE HOBOS!
FRANCIS!!

!!
FRANCIS!
COME BACK!
FRANCIS!

SSSHHHRRKK
AHHHH!

OOF!
FWUMP!

DARN, LOST IT...
BET IT'S AT THE END OF THIS RAVINE.

NUTS.
DID I GO BY HERE ALREADY?

WHOA.

RUSTLE
RUSTLE
RUSTLE

OOF!
THE HECK?!
FEELS LIKE WALKING THROUGH-

MOLASSES.
TICK TICK TICK TICK

THIS IS REALLY WEIRD.
TICK TICK
TICK
TICK TICK
TICK TICK

HUH?
TICK
TICK
TIIICK
TIIII'CK

TIICK
AAUGHH!!
TICK
TICK

WH-WHA-

WHO ARE YOU?!
TICK
TICK
FROM WHERE HAVE YOU COME?!

WHER-

AARGHH
BITE!

HAARRRGGHHHHH

HUFF

OW!
OUCH! OW!

A- A ROAD?
IN THE MIDDLE OF THE WOODS?

CLACK
CLACK
CLACK

HEY!
HEY, MISTER!

ARE... ARE YOU HEADED IN TO TOWN?
AYUP.
ROOM ON BACK.
SHIFT YOU QUICK.

MIND YOU DON'T RILE 'EM.
RILE WHAT?

CROOAKkkk

UM...
I THINK YOUR CHICKEN'S SICK, MISTER.
CROOOAAACKKKK

CRIMENY.
WHEN DID IT GET SO DARK?

CAN'T EVEN BE SIX YET...

BOY.
IN TOWN. STIR UP.

CROAAACKKK
...MMMPH.
WESTFIELD?
TOWN.

?

MMMMMMMMRRRRR

HISSSSSSS
SCREEEEE

HOLY-
MISTER! DIDJA SEE-
THAT.

EH?

NOW, WHERE-

AHHHH!!

HEY!!
WATCH WHERE-
MY WORD-
AHHHH

AAAAHHHHHHHHHHH
ACK!

AAAHHH!

AHHHHH!

–SO FRESH, THEY ARE BLEEDING–
UH-UH...

TEN FOR ONE!
DOESN'T JUST KILL LINDWORM
IT'S ROTTEN!
...
WHAT WOULD

OOOF!
BUMP!!
OI!
NOT TO RUN INTO US, STINKFISH.

AAHHHH!!

HUFF
HUFF

HUFF
HUFF
HUFF

?
CRNCHHHHHH
HISSSSSSS
HISSSSSSSSSSS
CRNNCHHHHH
SSSSSSCHRNCHHHHHH

HHISSSSSSSSSSS

AHHH!!

THIS ISN'T REAL.
I'M STILL IN BED. I'M STILL SLEEPING.

I'M DREAMING.

THIS IS ALL A DREAM.

!!

PLEASE LET THIS BE A DREAM.

THIS IS A DREAM.
IT'S ALL A DREAM
IT'S ALL A -
SCREEE!

WAKE UP, FRANCIS!
WAKE UP...

PLEASE WAKE UP.

PLEASE...

CREEEAAK
CREEAK
WHA-? WHERE-

HMMMPH. JUST AS I SUSPECTED.

THERE YOU ARE-

ARGHH!

WHA-
WHAT?
WHAT?!

GO AWAY!
GO AWAY!
YOU! GET OUT OF THERE!

GET OUT OR I'M CALLING THE WATCH!

LEAVE ME ALONE!!
LOOK, IF YOU'D JUST-
POLICE!
COME OUT-
HELP!
-I WON'T PRESS CHARGES.

DON'T TOUCH ME!
GET AWAY!
ACK!

STAY AWAY!
I'LL FIGHT YOU!
I WILL!
...ER.
YOU HAVE MY
PAPERS.
YOUR
WHAT?
MY PAPERS.
YOU'RE, AH, MAKING
THE PRINT RUN.
WHAT'S
WRONG WITH
YOUR EARS?

I WAS RATHER
ABOUT TO ASK YOU
THE SAME THING.
OH.
OH MY.
IS IT A
BIRTH
DEFECT?
WHAT?!

WHERE-
THIS IS
THE CIRCUS, RIGHT?
RIGHT?

...I NEED
TO USE THE
BATHROOM...

AHEM.
PLOP!

UM... THANKS, MISTER...?
FFRENSHE.
HUH?
FREN-SHAY. ELMERUGGE FFRENSHE.

THE WASHROOM'S THROUGH HERE.
DON'T TOUCH ANYTHING.
WHAT IS THIS PLACE?

A BOOKSTORE. OBVIOUSLY.
MIND THE SHELF.
WHEN DID WESTFIELD GET A BOOKSTORE?
I CAN'T SPEAK FOR THIS MR. WESTFIELD, WHOEVER HE-
NO, WESTFIELD THE TOWN. WHERE WE ARE.
RIGHT?

OH FOR-
WIPE YOUR FEET!

I'LL WASH MY SHOES IN THE BATHROOM, OKAY?
"SHOES?"
Y-YOUR FOOT JUST CAME OFF!

SO IF THIS ISN'T WESTFIELD, WHERE'S THIS? IT CAN'T BE GAINSBOROUGH-
I'VE NO IDEA WHAT YOU'RE SPEAKING OF. THIS IS THE WASHROOM.

SLAM
DO... DO YOU KNOW WHAT TOWN THIS IS?

VALLEYGHAST. NATURALLY.
WHERE IS "WESTFIELD"?
YOU KNOW. WEST OF THE FARMS.

WELL, AS THERE ARE NO TOWNS BUT AETHELGART AND GRYTHOM WITHIN A DAY'S TRAVEL, I DON'T KNOW WHERE YOU THINK YOU CAME FROM.

Hmmm... INTRIGUING.
FWOOOSH

'AETHELGART'? IS THAT DUTCH OR SOMETHING?
ARE YOU DERANGED?
YOU KEEP MAKING UP THESE BIZARRE NAMES-
FWOOOOSH!

YEAH, SURE...

WHAT ARE THESE THINGS?
HUH?
THESE THINGS THAT WERE ON YOUR FEET.
WHAT THINGS?
...SHOES?

HMMM. SHOES.

WHERE AM I?
KNOCK
KNOCK
KN-
OCK

KNOCK
KNOCK KNOCK KNOCK
OH BOY.

OH NO.
KNOCK
KNO

...NOT NOW...
KNOCK KNOCK
HISSSHH
HEY! I KNOW YOU'RE IN THERE!
OPEN UP!

BAM BAM BAM BA

HEY!

AHA!

SO THERE YOU ARE.

MORNING, ELM!
I BROUGHT BREAKFAST!

GOOD MORNING, KAY. I DON'T-
WELL, THINGS FOR BREAKFAST. BUT IT WON'T TAKE VERY LONG TO MAKE.

THAT'S REALLY NOT-
YOUR STOVE IS WORKING AGAIN, YES?
BARELY. LOOK-
OH! YOU KNOW MATHESIN, THE BAKER'S BOY?

KAY!

KAY-
WELL, I STOPPED BY- I WAS GOING TO THE MARKET, AND I NEEDED EMBROIDERY FLOSS-
SO, I SEE MATHESIN THERE, AND HE SAID HE SAW A MONSTER!
THIS IS NOT A GOOD TIME-
KAY, PLEASE.
IN THE MARKETPLACE LAST NIGHT!

MONSTER?

HE WAS OUT BUYING GREASE, SEE, AND AS HE CAME TO HIGH STREET-
THIS ISN'T THE MOST FORTUITOUS-
AND THEN-

THEN HE SEES THIS STRANGE LITTLE EARLESS CREATURE RUNNING ALL AROUND AND SCREAMING!
YOU SHOULD GO TALK TO HIM, GET THE STORY YOURSELF...
I'M BUSY.
OH, YOU AREN'T!
KAY.
DO YOU HAVE ANY GRINMEAL?
ER. NO.

KYNEBURGA, I INSIST THAT YOU-
I'LL JUST USE EXTRA LARD.

CREEEAAK

?

YOU DIDN'T SAY ANYTHING ABOUT HAVING COMPANY OVER!
I DON'T EXACTLY-
HONESTLY, ELM, YOU **COULD** SPEAK UP!
SLAM

WHAT ARE YOU DOING?
GO AWAY!
SSSCREECH!

CRASH
STOP DOING THAT!
NO!
...DO THEY NEED A DIGESTIVE TABLET?

ELM! IS THAT A CHILD?!
I-

...HARD TO EXPLAIN...
...WHY?...

...WHY DON'T YOU TELL ME...
...I TOLD YOU I AM BUSY AND I NEED...

I WEN-
WHUMP WH

OOOF!
FWUMP!

ARE YOU QUITE FINISHED?
...

AND YOU'RE COVERED IN SOOT...
WONDERFUL.
ELM?

WOULD YOU KINDLY PUT THAT DOWN, PLEASE?
OR YOU'LL WHAT?

OR I'LL BE WITHOUT AN EAR-PICK, I SUPPOSE.
OH, ICK!

WHAT... WHAT EXACTLY IS IT?
ON ITS WAY, ONE HOPES.

I FOUND IT UNDER THE STAIRS. KEEPS NATTERING ON ABOUT CIRCUSES AND A FIELD OR SOMESUCH.
IT'S... UM, A BIT UNUSUAL.
HEY! I GOT A NAME!

YOU'RE...
YOU'RE NOT VERY OLD, ARE YOU?
NO, MA'AM.

YOU DIDN'T SPEND THE NIGHT OUT THERE, DID YOU?
...YES'M.
WHERE'S YOUR HOME?
HAVE YOU BEEN TURNED OUT? ARE YOU LOST?

ELM, DIDN'T YOU HELP HIM?
LOOK, I ONLY FOUND HIM UNDER MY STOOP NOT FIVE MINUTES BEFORE YOU BARGED IN.

AND YOU DIDN'T EVEN ASK HIM WHO HE WAS?
WELL, NEITHER DID YOU-

ER.
WHAT IS YOUR NAME, LITTLE ... PERSON?

FRANCIS.
FRANCIS SHARP.

FRAHN-ZIS.
THAT'S... ORIGINAL!
I'M KYNEBURGA. KYNEBURGA GRUMENHULL.
AND YOU'VE ALREADY MET COUSIN ELMERUGGE, I EXPECT.
ER, QUITE.
I CALL HIM "ELM" FOR SHORT.
I WISH YOU WOULDN'T.

WELL, THAT'S INTRODUCTIONS.
YOU GET CLEANED, I'LL FINISH COOKING BREAKFAST-
AND YOU'LL BE ON YOUR WAY HOME WITH A MEAL INSIDE YOU!

AND YOU'RE NOT GOING TO EAT ME?
HA. HA.
ELM, WHAT HAVE YOU BEEN TELLING THIS CHILD?!

WELL, DON'T YOU WORRY, FRAHNZIS-
UM. FRANCIS.
WELL, DON'T YOU WORRY, FRANCIS. YOU'RE PERFECTLY SAFE WITH US!

CRUMBS! THE LARD!

OH! OHHHHH-
CLANG
CLATTER
WHOOMPF!
CLANG

AHEM.

HMMPH.

WASN'T IT COLD OUT THERE?
A BIT.
APPARENTLY HIS ESCAPADE IN THE MARKET LAST NIGHT LED HIM TO MY DOORSTEP.

UM.
I THOUGHT YOU SAID YOU WERE MAKIN' ROLLS.

THINGS GOT OUT OF HAND.
YOUR PORRIDGE IS FINE, AT LEAST.
IT'S BLACK.
WELL, YES!

SO, YOU'RE WITH A CIRCUS?
WHAT?! NO!
THEN WHY WERE YOU ASKING IF THIS WAS ONE?

ELM, SHUSH!
IT MIGHT BE A BIRTH DEFECT.
MAYBE THAT NO-GOOD CART DRIVER KIDNAPPED ME!
SNUCK ME AWAY TO JOIN THE CARNIES!
OTHER THAN THERE BEING NO CIRCUSES IN TOWN, A BRILLIANT DEDUCTION ON YOUR PART.

IN ANY CASE, WHAT WERE YOU DOING OUT IN THE WOODS AT NIGHT?
JUST CHASIN' SOME WEIRD CRITTER.
THEN THIS HOBO JUMPS ME-

A WHAT?!
-SO I BEAT IT TO THIS ROAD, AND THAT GUY COMES BY, AND HERE I AM...

THE OLD FOREST ROAD?
YOU KNOW WHERE I'M TALKING ABOUT?
QUITE. IT'S THE ONLY ROAD GOING THROUGH THE FOREST.
BACKTRACKING SHOULD BE SIMPLE.

SEE?
HOME AND DRY, EASY AS WISHING!

YOU'LL BE BACK WITH THE CIRCUS IN NO TIME!
KAY! THE BOWL-

SO. UM.
YOU LIVE IN YOUR STORE?
WELL, AFTER A FASHION.

IN FACT, I'VE BEEN AMASSING A SPECIALTY LIBRARY FOR MY OWN PERSONAL USE.
OCCASIONALLY, I AM FORCED TO SELL A BOOK HERE AND THERE.

MOST OF MY SPECIAL COLLECTION IS BACK HERE. TREATISES ON HISTORY, LANGUAGES, AND PARTICULARLY CRYPTOZOOLOGY.
ZOMBIE ANIMALS?

CRYPTOZOOLOGY IS THE STUDY OF BEASTS PURPORTED TO BE, AH, MYTHICAL.
A SCIENCE DENIED THE RESPECT AND APPLICABILITY OF PHRENOLOGY AND ALCHEMY, BUT NONETHELESS A SCIENCE STILL.

SO, YOU STUDY MADE-UP ANIMALS?

ANIMALS PURPORTED TO BE IMAGINARY, BUT WHICH ACTUALLY EXIST.
OH, LIKE BIGFOOT AND THE JERSEY DEVIL?
BIG... FOOT?

ER, WELL, I IMAGINE IT'S ALONG THOSE LINES, YES.
SO YOU LOOK FOR MAGIC THINGS, RIGHT?
THAT MAKES YOU LIKE THE OCCULTIST!
WHAT?!
DO YOU FIGHT CRIME AND STUFF?!

MY METHODOLOGY IS PRECISE AND LOGICAL. THE IDEA OF MAGIC IS ANATHEMA TO-
SO HAVE YOU EVER CAUGHT A BIGFOOT OR WHAT?!
ER... WELL.

WHILE I WOULD OF COURSE WELCOME THE OPPORTUNITY TO STUDY A LIVE SPECIMEN-
I FEAR I AM NOT MUCH OF A FIELD RESEARCHER.

BO-RING.
WELL, TO EACH HIS OWN.
ALTHOUGH-
I'VE GOT ONE SPECIMEN TO MY NAME.

BRACE YOURSELF. IT'S RATHER... UNORTHODOX.
I MYSELF CAN ONLY LOOK AT IT FOR SHORT PERIODS...

I'VE DESIGNATED IT AS THE LESSER BEFANGED SCRUB-TAIL.

IF ONE CONSIDERS THE PLACEMENT OF THE TARSUS IN ITS RELATION TO-
...

THERE YOU ARE! READY TO GO?
YES.
YES, I AM.
...AN ADAPTATION COMMONLY FOUND AM
THE LARGER BURROW
CREATURES, MAINLY

I RECKON MA WILL BE CRAZY BY NOW, ME BEING GONE-
MAYBE I CAN TELL HER I WAS WITH HARRY-

- AW, BUT THEY PROBABLY CHECKED WITH HIM. RATS!
HOPE HE DIDN'T FINK ON ME.
HIS EARS...

I'LL SPEAK WITH YOUR MOTHER. IT'LL BE FINE!
WITH ANY LUCK, SHE'LL JUST BE RELIEVED THAT YOU ARE SAFE!
YOU THINK SO?

HEY! WHERE'S MY BEDSHEET?
YOU MIGHT WANT TO WASH THIS AS SOON AS YOU'RE HOME.
ALTHOUGH...

HEY! WHAT-
BESIDES, THIS WILL PREVENT SOME EMBARRASSING QUESTIONS.
IT'S CHILLY.
A GUY WITH YOUR EARS, CALLIN' ME -

ALL SET!
PAT PAT

HONESTLY.
MAKE 'EM STAY AWAY!
H'SSSSSSSS

HEY, I CAME THROUGH HERE YESTERDAY!
THIS IS WHERE THE NIGHT MARKET SETS UP IN THE EVENING.
WHAT... WHAT KIND OF STUFF DO THEY SELL AT A NIGHT MARKET?
TUBERS, MOSTLY.

OKAY, THIS IS THE MAIN ROAD INTO TOWN. LOOK FAMILIAR?
YEAH! THAT GUY DROVE ME BY HERE-

-AFTER I MET THAT HOBO IN THE WOODS.
HEY!
WELL, THEN! BACK BY DINNERTIME!
I CAN'T BELIEVE IT! THIS IS GREAT-

HEY, CAN YOU TELL MY MA THAT I WAS HELPING YOU OUT OR SOMETHING?
SURE!
HELPING? WITH WHAT?
I DUNNO, WITH PATCHING A TIRE OR SOME-THING.
I DON'T WANT TO BE IN TROUBLE FOR BEING GONE ALL NIGHT-

SOMEHOW, I DOUBT THAT WILL BE BELIEVABLE.
C'MON, THROW ME A BONE!
WHY?
FINE. DON'T.

YEAH, GONNA BE GLAD TO SEE THE BACK OF YOU, FRENCHY.
FREHN-SHAY!

ALL RIGHT! I STOPPED HERE FOR A FEW SECONDS; I REMEMBER!
RIGHT AFTER I RAN OUTTA THAT CLEARING!
'CLEARING'? THERE'S AN OPEN SPACE NEAR HERE, RIGHT?

ER, YES.
ONE OF THE OLDER GROVES; ZAGREUS TREES MOSTLY.

WELL? C'MON!
LEAD THE WAY, FRENCHY.

SIGH.
STAY CLOSE.

WHAT IS IT, FRANCIS?
I CAME THROUGH HERE. IT WAS KIND OF DIFFERENT, BUT-

YEAH!

THIS IS IT!
I CAME THROUGH THESE TREES!

HOME AN' FREE!
WHOOo!

SLOW DOWN!
SHUSH, ELM. HE'S A CHILD.
HE JUST WANTS TO GO HOME.
YES, BUT WHERE EXACTLY IS THAT?

FINALLY!
I'M-

BACK.

THIS...
THIS ISN'T RIGHT.
MAYBE THEY BROKE CAMP.
ALTHOUGH, I DON'T SEE ANY TREADMARKS OR FIRE-

IT'S A FARM! A WHOLE FARM!
I'M NOT A CARNY! THERE IS NO CIRCUS!
ARE YOU SURE YOU WENT BY HERE?
YEAH, HARRY WAS BEHIND ME-

YOUR FRIEND, YES?
WE JUMPED THE FENCE AND-
-THE FENCE IS GONE!

AND THE FIELD... IT'S WAY TOO BIG.

WELL, IT'S OBVIOUS WHAT'S WRONG, THEN.
REALLY? WHAT?!
WE'RE IN THE WRONG LOCATION. WE-

THERE YOU ARE!

GAH!
OH, DID YOUR FAMILY LEAVE?
...NO.

NOT UNLESS THEY PACKED UP THE ENTIRE FARM AND THE ONE NEXT TO IT.
BUT I KNOW I CAME BY HERE!

THE WOODS ARE AWFULLY TWISTY.
BUT, NO FRETTING! COUSIN ELM AND ME HAVE WALKED UP HERE DOZENS OF TIMES. WE'LL GET YOU HEADED RIGHT IN LESS TIME THAN-
BUT KYN-KYNABURGER-

KYNEBURGA.
WHAT?
NOT 'BURGER', BURGA.
YEAH, OKAY.
OH WHAT?

NEVER MIND.

IT'S GETTING DARK.
WE SHOULD GET BACK TO TOWN.
...

BUT I SWEAR I CAME THROUGH HERE...

WELL, PERHAPS IF YOU DID SOME MENTAL BACKTRACKING.
YOU CAME THROUGH HERE, YOU MET SOMEONE-
SOMEONE. BUT I COULDN'T SEE WHO.
BECAUSE IT WAS DARK?

WELL, YEAH. BUT HE WAS ALL...
CREEPY.
AND THIS WAS WHEN?
YESTERDAY, AFTER LUNCH.
IT WAS DARK BY THEN?

BUT IT WASN'T. NOT 'TIL I RAN INTO THAT GUY! IT WAS ALMOST 3 O'CLOCK-
HEY!
MY WATCH!
WHERE'S MY WATCH!

WELL, NO SENSE IN LOOKING FOR IT NOW.
BUT-BUT I CAN'T GO BACK WITHOUT IT!
I JUST CAN'T!
WE DIDN'T THINK TO BRING A LANTERN AND WE'LL LOSE THE ROAD ONCE IT'S DARKER.
IN ANY CASE, YOU MOST LIKELY LEFT IT AT MY HOUSE.

...I JUST WANNA GO HOME...
YOU WILL. ELM AND ME BOTH, WE'LL GET YOU HOME.
ISN'T THAT RIGHT, ELM?

ER. YES. OF COURSE.
RIP!
AND THAT'S A PROMISE, FRANCIS!

CREEPY.
WHAT IS?

THE... TOWN. VALLEYGHAST.
WEIRD NAME.
IS IT? NOT THAT DIFFERENT FROM WEST... UM, WEST-
WESTFIELD.

FIELD, VALLEY; ALL THAT SORT OF THING.
I'M JUST SAYIN', WEIRD NAME EVEN FOR JERSEY.

WHO IS JERSEY?
KAY.
WERE YOU EXPECTING COMPANY?

WHAT?
NOT THAT I KNOW OF.

WELL, IT LOOKS AS THOUGH THEY ARE LEAVING.

IS SHE BEIN' ROBBED?
OF COURSE NOT.
CAN I CARRY THE TELESCOPE?
NO.

I DON'T WANNA GO HERE...
THIS IS THE FASTEST WAY THROUGH THE TOWN, SO-

IT'S SCARY!
PLEASE...
...FINE. WE'LL GO AROUND.

ELM, WE COULD TAKE THE ALLEY.

WHAT?! NO!
IT'S FAST, THERE'S STILL SOME LIGHT, AND THERE ARE THREE OF US. SHOULD BE FINE.
BUT-
LET'S JUST GET BACK, PLEASE?

THROUGH HERE.

I WENT THROUGH HERE!
WHAT IS THIS PLACE?
HISSSS

DUSTER'S ALLEY.
THE ONLY STREET THAT DOUBLES AS A LANDFILL.

I DON'T LIKE IT HERE...
THEN YOU'VE GOT SOME SENSE IN YOU.

FINALLY.
TIME FOR A CUP OF TEA, AT LEAST!
I'LL HELP FRANCIS SETTLE IN WITH YOU BEFORE I HEAD OFF, ELM.

WHAT?!
WELL, KYNEBURGA LIVES ALL THE WAY ACROSS TOWN. YOU MAY AS WELL STAY AT MY HOME-
BUT-

IN ANY CASE, I HAVE ALTERATIONS TO MAKE TO SOME GOWNS AND NEED TO WORK IN THE MORNING.
I'LL BE DONE BY THE TIME YOU'RE OPEN!
I'LL BE OPEN-

YOU'RE NEVER OPEN BEFORE TWELVE!
I DON'T WANNA STAY WITH HIM! HIS HOUSE SMELLS FUNNY!
THEN SLEEP UNDER THE STEPS AGAIN!

EVENING, MISS GRUMENHULL-
ELM, BE NICE-
-AND IT'S COLD, AND CREAKY-

...MISS?
I AM BEING-
I DON'T EVEN LIKE THIS GUY!
OH, THE TWO OF YOU!

IT'S MORE OF A CONCESSION THAN YOU KNOW.
TODAY'S BEEN NOTHING BUT MY HOME BEING INVADED-
AHEM.

TO BE CONTINUED...

MAXEEM KONRARDY
WWW.MAXEEM.COM

BARBARA GUTTMAN
WWW.MARTEANIART.COM